Highland Cattle

by E. Merwin

Consultant: Darin Collins, DVM
Director, Animal Health Programs
Woodland Park Zoo
Seattle, Washington

New York, New York

Credits

Cover, © Terry Whittaker/Minden Pictures; TOC, © Eric Isselee/Shutterstock; 4–5, © Jeffrey B. Banke/Shutterstock; 6–7, © defotoberg/Shutterstock; 8, © Bildagentur Zoonar GmbH/Shutterstock; 9T, © deaddogdodge/Dreamstime; 9B, © Boris Medvedev/Shutterstock; 10–11, © Avalon/Picture Nature/Alamy; 11R, © grafxart/Shutterstock; 12–13, © jpldesigns/Dreamstime; 14–15, © Amy Johansson/Shutterstock; 16, © Terry Whittaker/2020VISION/NPL/Minden Pictures; 17, © Astrid Gast/Dreamstime; 18L, © Volodymyr Burdiak/Shutterstock; 18–19, © Nick Garbutt/NPL/Minden Pictures; 20–21, © Klein and Hubert/Minden Pictures; 22 (T to B), © Paula Cobleigh/Shutterstock, © EcoPic/iStock, and © Leonardo Garofalo/Shutterstock; 23TL, © Jen Dunham/Shutterstock; 23TR, © Alistair Scott/Shutterstock; 23BL, © AZP Worldwide/Shutterstock; 23BR, © Adrien_G/Shutterstock.

Publisher: Kenn Goin
Senior Editor: Joyce Tavolacci
Creative Director: Spencer Brinker
Design: Debrah Kaiser
Photo Researcher: Thomas Persano

Library of Congress Cataloging-in-Publication Data

Names: Merwin, E., author.
Title: Highland cattle / by E. Merwin.
Description: New York, New York : Bearport Publishing, [2018] | Series: Even weirder and cuter | Audience: Ages 5–8. | Includes bibliographical references and index.
Identifiers: LCCN 2017039212 (print) | LCCN 2017052262 (ebook) | ISBN 9781684025251 (ebook) | ISBN 9781684024674 (library)
Subjects: LCSH: Highland cattle—Juvenile literature. | Cattle breeds—Juvenile literature.
Classification: LCC SF199.H54 (ebook) | LCC SF199.H54 M47 2018 (print) | DDC 636.2/23—dc23
LC record available at https://lccn.loc.gov/2017039212

Copyright © 2018 Bearport Publishing Company, Inc. All rights reserved. No part of this publication may be reproduced in whole or in part, stored in any retrieval system, or transmitted in any form or by any means, electronic, mechanical, photocopying, recording, or otherwise, without written permission from the publisher.

For more information, write to Bearport Publishing Company, Inc., 45 West 21st Street, Suite 3B, New York, New York 10010. Printed in the United States of America.

10 9 8 7 6 5 4 3 2 1

Contents

Highland Cattle 4

More Weird Cattle 22

Glossary. 23

Index 24

Read More 24

Learn More Online 24

About the Author 24

What are these weird but cute animals?

Long horns!

They're **Highland cattle.**

Highland cattle look cuddly and cute.

Yet these animals are tough.

They can survive in cold, windy places.

Look at all that hair!

These furry cattle are colorful.

Their coats can be black, red, yellow, white, or **brindle**.

Imagine a grand piano—that's how much a Highland **bull** can weigh!

Highland cattle have two layers of hair.

The warm inner layer is short and fluffy.

The long outer layer keeps the animals dry.

Highland cattle have extra-long eyelashes. They shield the animals' eyes from flying bugs.

Both male and female Highland cattle have horns.

On females, or cows, the horns curve upward.

On bulls, they're straighter.

male

A group of Highland cattle is called a fold.

Highland cattle put their long horns to work!

In winter, they use them to dig under snow.

The animals find frozen plants to munch on.

The Highland's horns keep growing throughout the animal's life.

These calm cattle love being around people.

Highland cattle can live for about 20 years.

Long ago, Scottish families kept their cows inside their homes on cold nights!

Highland calves are small at birth.

They slurp down their mother's **nutritious** milk.

The fuzzy babies grow quickly.

Watch out!

Highland cattle are very **protective**.

The whole group works together to keep the babies safe.

Cows sometimes hide their calves if danger is near.

More Weird Cattle

Ankole-Watusi Cattle
These long-horned cattle come from Africa. Their amazing horns can grow up to 8 feet (2.4 m) long!

Brahman Cattle
These strange-looking cattle have floppy ears and a big hump. They come from India, where they are thought to be holy.

Chianina Cattle
Chianina cattle from Italy top the charts for weight. A bull can weigh more than 3,800 pounds (1,724 kg). That's more than 10 refrigerators!

Glossary

brindle (BRIN-duhl) a fur color with streaks of dark and light hairs

bull (BUL) an adult male belonging to the cattle family

nutritious (noo-TRISH-uhs) providing substances that make a body healthy

protective (pruh-TEK-tiv) keeping something safe

Index

babies 18–19, 21
bulls 9, 12–13, 22
cows 4–5, 12–13, 17, 18–19, 20–21
eyelashes 11
hair 4, 8–9, 10–11
horns 4–5, 12–13, 14–15, 22
milk 18–19
Scotland 7, 17
size 9, 22

Read More

Carraway, Rose. *Cows on the Farm (Farm Animals).* New York: Gareth Stevens (2012).

Doyle, Sheri. *Cows (Farm Animals).* North Mankato, MN: Capstone (2013)

Learn More Online

To learn more about Highland cattle, visit
www.bearportpublishing.com/EvenWeirderAndCuter

About the Author

E. Merwin is a writer who much admires the calm and gentle nature of the powerful creatures known as Highland cattle.